mail-order brides books

Maryanne makes a detour
Interrupted Bridal Journey
Part One
By: Kent Hamillton[1]

---

1. https://www.amazon.com/s/ref=dp_by-line_sr_ebooks_1?ie=UTF8&text=Kent+Hamillton&search-alias=digital-text&field-author=Kent+Hamillton&sort=relevancerank

Chapter 1

Maryanne opened the letter carefully, and smoothed it out on the table. She began reading.

Dear Maryanne,

I am most pleased to make your acquaintance. As you will see from the letterhead, my name is Thomas Worthington, and I live in San Francisco.

I am a cloth manufacturer and have my own factory which is doing reasonably well. I am 37 years old, and have never been married. This has been mainly due to my spending my time building up my business.

However, I now find that the business doesn't require my full attention, and the need for a feminine influence in my life is becoming apparent. Plus I am becoming aware of the fact that I shall require an heir.

This was the motivation for my contacting Brides By Mail, who put your name forward as a possible wife for me.

They included a photograph in their letter to me, and you seem to be what I am searching for.

I offer you a secure life, free from financial stresses, a large house to run, with servants for the menial chores, and the prospect of having children after an appropriate interval.

Should you accept my offer, kindly reply to this letter. I shall then arrange to wire funds to you for your journey to San

MARYANNE MAKES A DETOUR INTERRUPTED BRIDAL JOURNEY

Francisco, and other sundries as may be necessary to affect your move. You will be accommodated in a separate part of my house while wedding arrangements are being made, and once married we shall share the main quarters.

I await your reply.

I am, Yours Truly, Thomas Worthington, Esq.

    Maryanne sat and looked at the letter. "He does sound a bit stuffy, don't you think, Mr. Tibbles?" She tickled the cat, who replied with an assenting purr. "But a life of relative ease; that's not to be dismissed lightly! Let's ask Aunt Hilda what she thinks."
    Maryanne's parents had died while she was young, and she had been raised by her aunt. She, however, had rather narrow views on Maryanne's socializing with the opposite sex, resulting in Maryanne's reaching the age of 23 without any suitors even knowing about her, let alone asking for her hand. For this reason she had decided to contact Brides By Mail. Her aunt had been initially against the idea, but she eventually saw that trying to stop the girl from having a normal life was simply being selfish on her own part, and she had finally assented to the idea.
    "Aunt, I have received an offer from a gentleman in San Francisco. Tell me what you think." She gave her aunt the letter.
    Aunt Hilda finished reading the letter. She put it down, and then looked at Maryanne. "As much as I shall miss having you around, I do feel it is the best for you. It would seem that he will provide for you handsomely."
    "Yes, aunt, but what about love? What about passion? This letter is as dry as dust. And he doesn't even include a photograph of himself! What if I don't like the way he looks?"
    "Child, love and passion flare up for a short time, and then you are left with the day to day business of life together. It would be nice to begin with love and passion, but if that doesn't happen, that is a small price to

pay for a secure life. Your parents started out with so much love and passion that I was almost jealous of your mother. But it didn't last; it never does. And once they were simply left with each other, and no money to speak of, life became hard. They fought about money almost constantly. Their initial love and devotion didn't stop that. And it was a combination of their penniless state, and their constant warring that contributed to their early deaths. Compare their lives with mine. Your uncle, may he rest in peace, and I never had a day of passion in our lives together, but we had security, and without the constant worry of money, we built up respect and acceptance for each other."

"Respect and acceptance! That sounds so dull! Did you not have any male friends before you met uncle?"

Her aunt looked at her sharply. "I may have, but that is not under discussion right now. I would advise you to consider this offer favorably. Another one like it may not come along for a long time, if at all."

"What do you think, Mr. Tibbles?" enquired Maryanne of the cat. Mr. Tibbles looked at her with his usual non-comprehending look. While thinking "As long as my food bowl is filled every morning, I really don't care what you do!"

Maryanne went and sat on the window seat, and looked out at the gray day. There was a lot of sense in what her aunt said, but at the same time she wished for something more. She had just finished reading *Far From the Madding Crowd*, and she could not but see Thomas Worthington in the character of Farmer Boldwood. While not exactly putting herself into the role of Bathsheba, she certainly saw the attraction of someone like Sergeant Troy. Someone who was interesting, impulsive, even a little dangerous, but who brought passion to life.

She thought longingly "Can't I just have a little love and passion before settling down?"

Chapter 2

Maryanne slept on the offer, and pondered upon it. Her aunt had brought her up to be sensible and thoughtful, and after a few days she decided that it would be the sensible thing to accept.

She sat down to write to her future husband.

>Dear Mr. Worthington...

Too formal. She scrunched the paper up and threw it away.

>Dear Thomas...

No, that was too forward. She had not even met him yet! She threw that one away too.

>Dear Mr. Worthington,
>Thank you for your kind offer of marriage.
>I have considered it carefully, and have decided to accept.
>I look forward to meeting you, and eventually making you a good wife.
>Yours etc.

She thought that if she wrote in the same rather formal and passionless way that his letter had been written, it would please him and smooth their path together. It would not have been appropriate to ask for love and passion when it was reasonably obvious that there was none to be had.

She included details that he would need for the money transfer, sealed it all in an envelope, and placed it on her bedside table.

That night she dreamed that she was now married to Mr. Worthington (she even called him that in her dream). And he DID look exactly like she had imagined Mr. Boldwood to look! They lived in a huge mansion, and there were servants scurrying to and fro everywhere. She could not do anything without a servant jumping to do it for her. It quickly became impossible. If she wanted to write a letter to someone, a servant would whisk the pen and paper away from her and begin writing. If she wanted to read a book, a servant would gently remove the book from her hand and begin reading to her. It became ridiculous. A servant saw her sitting at the window, looking out at the garden, and told her that he would rather look out the window for her, to save her the trouble!

At that point she woke up and lay there wondering about the dream. Could having servants doing all the menial work become irksome? Her aunt had a maid who did cooking and cleaning, but many of the other chores were shared between her and her aunt. She didn't find them to be a bother, and she actually derived some pleasure from doing them well. If she had nothing to do, would she be able to be satisfied with a life of leisure? She came to no definite conclusion.

She posted the letter the next day, and carried on her life as before. A few weeks later a reply arrived from Thomas Worthington.

> My Dear Maryanne,
>
> Your reply has filled my heart with gladness!
>
> I am sure you will be very happy here. Every desire of yours, within reason, will be accommodated, and you will have comforts aplenty.
>
> I have arranged to wire sufficient funds to cover your train journey from Baltimore to San Francisco, plus extra for any new clothes that you may require for the journey, and other incidentals.
>
> Kindly contact the Pacific Railroad Company to book your ticket, and inform me of the date of your arrival.

In the meantime I shall instruct the servants to perform a full house cleaning, and specifically the rooms that you will occupy before the wedding.

I reiterate my happiness at your acceptance!

Yours etc.

At least he showed an ability to experience happiness, Maryanne thought; he's not totally devoid of emotion. But still no mention of love or passion. She supposed it was maybe not fair to require love and passion, when Thomas (she made a mental effort to start thinking of him by his first name) had not even met her yet in the flesh, but it would have been pleasant to have a bit more fire in his letter.

The next day she went to the Western Union office to get the money Thomas had wired. She was amazed to discover that he had sent her $300! Way more than was required for a ticket and incidentals.

She then went to the train station, and enquired about trains to San Francisco.

"We have a five day cross-country Pullman service, that leaves every Friday." the clerk told her. "You can have your own compartment, or you can share with other women. Your own costs more. There is a dining car, and the ticket includes three meals a day."

Maryanne decided that with the amount that Thomas had sent her, she could easily afford to have a compartment to herself. Not only did she not have any male friends, but she did not even really have any female friends of her own, and she was not used to spending time in the company of other people, other than her aunt. She had had quite a sheltered upbringing.

Finally the day arrived that she was to leave. She packed the last few things in her trunk, and the two men who were to cart it and them to the station fetched it and placed it in their wagon.

She and Aunt Hilda got into the wagon for the short trip to the station.

"I hope that you are very happy with Mr. Worthington. Let me see, how does it sound: 'Maryanne Worthington'! Very respectable! I am sure that, as long as you look at the entirety of life with him, you will be very happy. He may not sweep you off your feet, but that is overrated anyway!"

"Thanks, aunt. Yes, 'Maryanne Worthington' sounds fine to me too! Don't worry, I shall do my best to make this marriage work. And since it seems I shall be well-to-do, I shall be able to come and see you every so often. Will you be OK without me?"

"Yes, child, I shall be fine. The house will be quieter, no doubt, but Mr. Tibbles and I shall look after each other quite all right."

Maryanne noticed a small tear on her aunt's cheek, and she suddenly hugged her. They had not had a very demonstrative relationship ever, but now, as they were about to part for who knew how long, they hugged each other close.

They parted, and Aunt Hilda blew her nose. "I'm just being silly! I'll see you again soon! Don't worry about me!"

The men carried the trunk through to the platform, and took it to the baggage car. Maryanne and her aunt said their final goodbyes, and Maryanne went to climb aboard. As she did so, she noticed that there were a number of soldiers further down the platform, also busy embarking. She wondered idly why they were there.

Chapter 3

The train pulled out of Baltimore and slowly picked up speed. Maryanne watched the city going by, and gradually thinning out as they left it behind.

Oh well, she thought, phase one of my life is over! I wonder what phase two will bring.

She settled into her compartment. It had almost everything that she needed in what was a very small room. There were two bunks facing each other, one of which converted into a bed. A small table that could fold up out of the way was between them.

She spent the rest of the afternoon reading and updating her diary. It was not always easy to write, what with the constant movement of the train.

Finally, at 6pm, the time they had told her dinner would be served in the dining car, she left her compartment and made her swaying way along the train. At times, as it lurched particularly badly, she used the side of the corridor for support. She wondered if this was what it was like to be drunk.

She reached the dining car, and the maître d' asked her whether she would be prepared to share a table with another couple. She agreed gladly - she was already feeling a little lonely.

The maître d' checked with a middle-aged couple at a table further down the car, who seemed to assent, and he came back and led her to the table. The man stood up, as well as he was able, and bowed to her. "Good evening madam! You are more than welcome to share our table. I am George, and this is my wife Martha. We are the Thackerays."

"Thank you very much. My name is Maryanne Marston." She sat down.

After a minute or two, during which she made her selections from the menu, George addressed her. "So, what is a young woman like you doing crossing this great land of ours alone?" he enquired.

Maryanne saw no reason to be coy about the reason for her journey. "I am on my way to meet my future husband. I am what is known as a mail-order bride."

George's eyebrows shot up, and Martha's eyes opened wide. They were not quite sure what to make of this information.

"Indeed!" exclaimed George. "I had heard of these arrangements, but I have never actually met someone who was undertaking them. May I enquire - please refrain from answering if you would rather not - why you embarked upon this rather unusual method of finding a husband? You are, if I may say so," and here he looked rather nervously at his wife, "quite attractive, and you are obviously educated, so I would have thought that finding a suitable suitor would not have been that difficult."

Maryanne saw no reason not to carry on with her candid admissions. "I was orphaned quite young, and my aunt raised me. Whether she was trying to protect me, in an area in which she felt my parents had failed, or whether she simply didn't see the need for my having an active social life, I'm not quite sure. But I grew up with a very limited circle of acquaintances, amongst which were no suitable men. However, I decided that the life of a spinster did not have great attractions, and so the only other avenue available, that I could see, was this one."

George and Martha digested this information carefully.

Martha spoke. "I think that's a wonderful thing! For a woman to take charge of her life and plot its course on her own - good for you! Too many women these days take whatever life dishes up to them, without striking out in their own direction. I take my hat off to you! Who knows, if I hadn't met George, I might have done the same as you. If these services had existed then. Who is the lucky young man?"

"He's a little bit older than me" said Maryanne. "He's a manufacturer in San Francisco."

"Really!" said George. "May we know his name?"

"Thomas Worthington."

"Bless my soul! We know him well! Who would have guessed!" They all pondered the coincidence that had presented itself. "I may say, without giving too much away, that you are headed for a comfortable life. Thomas's business has done very well, and he will be able to keep you in a way to which I am sure you will easily become accustomed."

"Tell me a bit about him!" asked Maryanne. "His letters were quite formal, and he didn't go into any detail about himself at all."

Martha resumed. "He is a hard worker, and a good man all round. Salt of the earth. I'm sure you'll like him."

Maryanne was painfully aware that Martha made no mention of anything passionate about his nature. He sounded very stolid. And Martha had said 'like', not 'love'.

She was tempted to ask them what it was that had made Thomas decide on a mail-order bride, but thought better of it. It wasn't really their place to surmise on Thomas's reasons, and even if they knew them, it might have been considered disloyal to their friend to mention them to her, who was, at this point anyway, still a stranger to them all.

Maryanne and the couple chatted amiably through the rest of their meal, and they told her what life was like in San Francisco. At least the life there sounded like it was more interesting than where she had come from. Hopefully the environment in which she lived would provide her with some sort of dissipation, even if her home life promised to be rather plain.

After dessert she thanked them for their hospitality and excused herself, and walked back down the dining car on her way to her compartment.

The soldiers that she had noted on the station when she was leaving Baltimore, were sitting at the tables she was passing, and she couldn't help noticing that more than one of them surreptitiously threw an admiring glance at her. She had not been in that many situations where men would admire her, and she found it not altogether unpleasant.

Chapter 4

Maryanne found it surprisingly easy to sleep on the train. The rocking motion was rhythmic, and was not unlike a mother rocking her baby. And although the train was not quiet, the noise was constant and also rhythmic, so after a while one was not even aware of it. She awoke refreshed.

At breakfast George and Martha, and the soldiers, were nowhere to be seen. She ate alone.

She watched the countryside going by. They were in a very deserted area; she assumed it was some part of Indiana. She had perused the route that the train would be taking, when she bought her ticket.

After breakfast she returned to her compartment, and settled in to read her book. After a short while, the train lurched to what seemed to her, a rather sudden stop. She wondered what the cause was.

She opened the window and put her head out to see. A second later, there was a loud crack, and the wood above her head splintered. At the same time, the compartment door was flung open and one of the soldiers, holding a rifle, rushed into the compartment and pulled her in from the window. "Get down on the floor!" he shouted at her. He then looked carefully out the window, before loosing off a couple of shots himself. Maryanne had never heard anything as loud as the noise of the rifle. Her ears were ringing. At that, the train started up again, and picked up speed quite quickly. The soldier kept a vigil at the window for another minute or two, before turning to look at Maryanne.

"You can get up now!" he smiled. "Sorry about that! I didn't have time for explanations! If you'd stayed there, who knows, their next shot might have found its target!"

"Thank you! Who was that, that was shooting at the train?" Maryanne resumed her seat.

The soldier, without any invitation, sat down on the bunk opposite her. "Shawnees. There are still small pockets of them resisting white settlement. They put a rock on the line to make the train stop, and then they were going to ambush it. But they hadn't bargained on getting the reception that they did! We were waiting for them. This stretch has this sort of thing happen occasionally, and that's why we are here, to protect you fine folk!"

"I wondered why there were soldiers on the train."

"I heard the shot, just as I was passing your compartment, and I saw that they were shooting at you. So I decided that the last thing I wanted was to have a bullet mar that pretty face!"

Maryanne blushed slightly.

"We saw you at dinner last night. Was that your parents you were sitting with?"

"No, I met those people only then myself! I am travelling alone."

"Really! Leaving your husband, or returning to your husband? Whoops, sorry, I am forgetting my manners." He stood up. "I am Peter Simpson. How do you do?" He bowed, and extended his hand to take hers.

"How do you do? I am Maryanne Marston." Peter kissed her hand lightly, and reseated himself.

Maryanne found his rather forward questioning a little unusual, but she was not used to dissembling to people, so she answered plainly. "Neither, actually. Well, he's not my husband yet, anyway. I am travelling to meet my future husband. I am a mail-order bride."

Peter bent forward and looked at her keenly. "Why, in all the world, would someone as pretty as you need to be a mail-order bride?"

Maryanne gave the same basic explanation that she had to the couple at dinner the previous evening.

"You mean there were no real males, in your vicinity that had the gumption to ask for your hand! I had always wondered about the so-called men of Baltimore. They are living up to their reputation! If I had been around, that situation would have been different! Mail-order bride! This is a travesty!"

Maryanne wasn't sure whether she should be upset at what Peter was saying. But she supposed that he was casting aspersions more on the men of her home town, than on her. She decided to give him the benefit.

"And who is this lucky man that is waiting for you at the end of the line?"

"Thomas Worthington. He is a successful business owner."

"Never heard of him. Why does HE need to order a bride by mail order? Why can't he find a woman locally?" Maryanne bridled a little at that, and Peter checked himself. "Sorry, that is not really my business. I withdraw the question!" he said with a smile.

"Well, if you really want to know, he has been building his business for the last few years, and has not been able to take time out to seek a wife." Maryanne found herself almost needing to apologize for Thomas.

"Hmm. Those sorts of men might become married, but their business remains their mistress! After not having time for a woman for so many years, I hope he manages to find the time for you!"

Maryanne shrugged. "Possibly not as much as I should like, but the ease of life will compensate for that. He seems to be very well-off."

"You think that money can make up for love? I'm afraid I can't agree! Love is all that is worth fighting for. Money simply keeps you warm at night."

Maryanne replied "I have no experience of either, so I'll take what you say under advisement."

Peter stood up. He looked down at her. "I call it criminal that a woman like you might never know real love, real passion! Au revoir!" and he left.

Maryanne sat there, thinking about what he had said. His final remark echoed through her head, and gnawed at her resolve.

Chapter 5

When it came time for lunch, Maryanne wended her way to the dining car as before. As she entered, she saw George and Martha at their table, and she began walking to it. However, she almost immediately found her way blocked by Peter Simpson.

"My dear Miss Marston, would you be so good as to grace our table with your presence?" She could not decide whether he was teasing her or not, with his exaggerated speech. There were two other soldiers at the table with him, who both stood up.

"Please, we would be honored," the one said.

"It would make our day!" said the other.

The Thackerays hadn't actually noticed her arrival yet, and so she decided that there could be no harm. She sat down. The rest of them sat down. The other two soldiers were introduced by Peter as Stephen and Andrew.

Maryanne addressed the other two. "So, who did you two rescue this morning, while Peter here was holding the entire Shawnee nation at bay on my behalf?" She had decided that, if Peter was going to exaggerate, she could match him.

"Oh, no such derring-do on our part, I'm afraid," Stephen said. "We just gave cover to the engineer who had to go and remove the rocks from the line. Saw one or two of them in the distance, but they were no real threat. But I believe Peter had to pull you in from the window! He's so rough!" he said with a grin.

"Yes, I know," said Maryanne. "I still have the bruises!"

Peter laughed. "I did apologize afterwards, remember! Rather a bruise than a bullet, don't you think?"

"Yes, indeed," said Maryanne.

The four of them made polite conversation for a few minutes more, and then Stephen and Andrew got up to leave. "Please excuse us."

Stephen said. "We had already eaten when you arrived, and we need to attend to some things." They went and left Peter and Maryanne alone.

"So you're going all the way through to San Francisco," mused Peter. "We'll be leaving the train at Omaha."

"Oh, why is that?" asked Maryanne.

"We are based in Omaha. We leave the train, and another platoon takes over from Omaha to the coast. We go back to our barracks, and then get on the train again on its way back East."

"I see. And what do you do in your barracks while waiting for the train to return?"

"Play cards. Polish our boots. Clean our kit. Occasionally we are required to go on patrols in areas where the Indians are up to something, but generally we have a lot of time to spare. But enough about me. I want to find out more about you."

"I am not very interesting, I am afraid."

"Oh, I am sure you are. You just don't know all the things about you that I shall find interesting! Where were you born?"

"In Baltimore."

"You said earlier that you were orphaned, and that you had a rather secluded upbringing with your aunt."

"Oh, so you remember what I told you!"

"Oh yes, I remember everything you told me! But did you not have ANY men friends? To take you to balls, the opera, concerts, that sort of thing?"

"No, nothing like that. Occasionally my aunt and I would go to a concert, or the opera, but I never went with a man."

"Hm. I can't help feeling that you need to see a little more of life before you settle down with the worthy Mr. Worthington."

"Oh you do, do you? You know about these things?"

"Indeed I do. And I happen to know exactly the right man to do it!"

Maryanne was not so inexperienced as to misunderstand his offer. She just looked at him and smiled.

MARYANNE MAKES A DETOUR INTERRUPTED BRIDAL JOURNEY

"Come, finish your dessert, and then I want to show you something," Peter said.

Chapter 6

She finished eating, and they got up. By now George and Martha had noticed her. She waved at them, and they waved back. They watched her and Peter departing together, for a little longer than was required.

Peter led her into the next car, and along the length of its corridor. As they reached the coupling between that car and the following one, he stopped. They were standing between the cars, with the countryside rushing past on either side.

"Right, follow me," he said. He began climbing up the ladder on the end of the one car. Maryanne looked slightly alarmed. But she followed him anyway. He reached the top, and heaved himself onto the top of the car. She climbed up until her head was higher than the roof of the car. The wind rushing past tousled her hair.

"I can't get on top there, it's too high!" she shouted, to be heard above the wind.

"I'll help you!" he shouted back.

Peter found purchase with his foot on a jutting out part of the roof, and then part helped, and part pulled Maryanne on to the top of the car. She knelt facing the direction they were moving, with the wind blowing her hair around her face. Then she turned to sit next to him.

They sat there, watching the smoke rise from the engine at the front, the grass and trees rushing past on either side, all the way to the distant mountains. She had never felt so alive in her life. She whooped with joy. "I've never done anything like this before!" she shouted at Peter. For some reason that she could not fathom, she was not afraid.

"We're just getting started!" he replied.

After a minute or two of sitting like this, the train went around a gentle curve, and up ahead they suddenly saw a tunnel. "What do we do now?" she shouted.

"You lie face down. And keep your eyes and mouth shut!"

"Why?"

MARYANNE MAKES A DETOUR INTERRUPTED BRIDAL JOURNEY

"You'll see!"

Peter crawled a short distance away from her, and then lay face down on the roof, facing the front. She did the same, where she was, and raised her head to watch the tunnel get closer and closer. As the engine went into the tunnel, she suddenly understood the reason for Peter's advice. Without the open air around it, the smoke from the engine was now confined inside the tunnel. As they went into the tunnel she dropped her head and closed her mouth and eyes tight. The noise, which had been considerable before, now became deafening, as the sound of the engine, the wind and the noise of the car itself, all reverberated inside the tunnel. But what was most amazing to her was smoke from the engine. It was both hot, and full of little particles of soot. As she lay there the hot smoke and the soot swirled around her, and she could feel the soot touching her skin and even getting into her ears. It was a sensory excess.

Finally she heard the sound from the engine diminish, and she realized that it was back in the open. She kept her head down, and a few seconds later she saw sunlight again behind her eyelids, and opened her eyes. Raising her head, she could not stop laughing. "That was amazing! I think I've got soot everywhere!" she shouted at Peter.

He returned to where she was. "You have it in your hair, and all over your face!" he laughed.

"So do you!" she returned. The strange thing about the soot was that it didn't smudge and leave streaks on her skin. The particles were hard, and could be brushed off quite easily. After another minute or two in the wind, most of the soot in her hair and on her face had been blown off.

"Have you had enough?" he asked.

"Yes, OK."

She crawled backwards to the ladder, and with his help managed to work her way over the edge and get her footing on it again. She climbed back down, shortly followed by Peter. They stood there laughing.

"That was the strangest thing I've done in my life!" she said. "I suppose you do it every trip!"

"No, actually, not. I have been on top of the car before, but it's the first time I've been through a tunnel."

"So how did you know it was safe! What if the gap between the car and the roof of the tunnel had been too small, and we had been swept off the car?"

"I didn't know. There was not enough time to get down from the roof when we saw the tunnel, so I took a chance. Carpe Diem! But I knew about the smoke from times I've been into a tunnel with the compartment window open." He looked at the side of her head. "You have a whole tender of coal in your ears! You'd better go and wash. But please don't do anything with your hair! The wind has teased it into a magnificent frame for your face!"

"I don't believe you! It's you who's teasing me!" She felt her hair with her hand, and it seemed to have twice the volume it usually had.

"OK, you go back to your compartment, and sort yourself out. I'll be along in half an hour to show you something else."

And so they parted, with Maryanne wondering what Peter planned to show her next.

Chapter 7

She returned to her compartment, and washed her face and ears, brushed her hair, and changed her dress. The one she had been wearing was scuffed with dirt from crawling around on the roof. She then tried to read, but could not concentrate on her book, so she sat watching the trees rush past.

Promptly after half an hour, there was a knock on her door. Peter stood there, with his rifle. He came into the compartment, and sat down, leaving the door open.

"Have you ever used a firearm?" he asked.

"No" replied Maryanne.

"Would you like to give it a try?"

"Why not? This is not turning out to be a normal day in any other way, so why stop now?"

Peter gave her a quick lesson on the different parts of the rifle, and how to hold it, with the butt against her shoulder, and to look along the sights. He helped her get it into position by putting his arms around her shoulders and supporting its weight while she settled herself under it. She was acutely aware of his proximity; she had never been so close to a man before. He released his hold on the rifle and allowed her to take its full weight.

He opened the window. "OK, fire away when you're ready. Just keep the butt pressed hard into your shoulder!"

She squinted down the sights, and aimed at a tree passing in the distance, and squeezed the trigger. She knew that it was going to be loud, from Peter's firing it during the ambush, but with her ear that much closer to it now, the noise was incredible. Plus, the kick back into her shoulder was violent.

She lowered the rifle, and handed it back to Peter. "Thanks, once is enough! How does your shoulder take all that punishment?" she said, massaging her shoulder ruefully.

"You get used to it." He removed the magazine and made the rifle safe, and then propped it against the wall of the compartment.

He rummaged in his pocket and brought out a pack of cards. He shuffled them, and then fanned them out towards her. "Take any card, look at it without showing me, and then replace it anywhere you like."

She did as instructed. He shuffled the cards again, and then fanned them towards himself. He removed one, and showed it to her. "This was your card."

Her eyes widened. "How did you do that?"

"A magician never divulges his secrets! You'd have to torture me."

"That could be arranged!"

He smiled. "If I were going to be tortured, I cannot imagine anyone I would rather have torture me than you!"

Maryanne blushed.

MARYANNE MAKES A DETOUR INTERRUPTED BRIDAL JOURNEY

Maryanne and Peter spent the rest of the afternoon together. He told her stories of his exploits as a soldier, and she listened with growing enchantment. He pointed out interesting landmarks that they were passing, and related incidents that had happened there, where he knew the details. He had a smattering of botanical knowledge too, and he showed her some of the trees and flowers that he knew. They saw a herd of bison at one stage, and they watched them and marveled at their size and powerful build.

Maryanne found him to be interesting and stimulating. She had never known that the company of someone else could be such fun. He left her late in the afternoon, and she decided not to eat in the dining car this evening, but to take a small meal in her compartment. Within a short time of his leaving her, she found that she was missing his company. She wondered whether this was normal so soon after meeting a person.

She tried to read, but after re-reading the same sentence five times, without comprehending anything, she gave up and watched the sunset. Her mind was in a whirl.

Chapter 8

That night Maryanne did not sleep well. She wondered whether it was the rocking of the train, but that had not prevented her from sleeping well the first night. She knew that she was severely troubled.

In the short time she had known Peter Simpson, she had realized that a man could be fun to be with, could be interesting and stimulating. Peter was all these things, and when she compared him with the sort of man that Thomas Worthington had projected himself to be, via his letters, she found Peter by far the more attractive person.

She decided to try and winkle more information out of the Thackerays. She went to breakfast, and luckily they were there, and Peter was not. She asked if she might join them again, and they assented gladly.

After giving her order to the steward, and after waiting what seemed an appropriate interval so as not to make it seem that it was the primary purpose of her visit, she asked "Tell me a little more about Thomas. What sort of person is he? Is he fun to be with?"

Martha immediately knew where Maryanne was coming from. Her feminine instinct understood exactly what was going on. George, as with most males, was blissfully unaware of Maryanne's real reason, and took her question at face value. He replied, "Fun to be with is a bit strong to describe him. He's pleasant, and he knows a lot about cloth." Maryanne nodded.

Martha was faced with a dilemma. Should she sell Thomas hard, and paint a glamorous picture of him for Maryanne? Or should she tell it like it is, that Thomas was decidedly not fun to be with, but was a good man nonetheless. She tried to steer a middle path. "Thomas is interesting in his own way, and once you get to know that way, you will find him good company."

Maryanne, however, for all her naïveté, could see right through what Martha was saying. She had her fair share of feminine intuition too. To her, it shouted "Dull, dull, dull!"

MARYANNE MAKES A DETOUR INTERRUPTED BRIDAL JOURNEY

They made desultory conversation for the rest of the meal, and Maryanne returned to her compartment to agonize.

She realized that she was not actually sure what she was agonizing about, other than whether to carry on to San Francisco and her fate with Thomas Worthington. Peter had not made any suggestion, or any sort of offer, so it was not as if there was a clear alternative. She was just coming to the inescapable conclusion that she could not carry on with the marriage arrangement with Thomas. With people like Peter in the world, the Thomas's didn't stand a chance.

There was a knock at her door. She opened it, and Peter stood there. "Good morning, Miss Muffett! How did you sleep?"

"Passing well, thank you. And you?"

"Wonderfully! May I come in?"

She retreated into the compartment. Peter came in, and this time closed the door behind him.

He sat on the bunk opposite her, and looked at her. He didn't say anything. She returned his gaze levelly.

He looked out the window, and suddenly seemed to get an idea. He went to it, opened it and looked out. They were at that stage passing through a cutting, where there was bushy vegetation growing up the bank, quite close to the train line. He waited for a few seconds, and then lunged outward. He came away from the window with a flower in his hand. He closed the window, and sat down again. He looked at her.

"Maryanne..."

She waited. She looked at him.

"Maryanne, this may seem totally precipitate, and I suppose it is. Since the moment I set eyes upon you, I have felt this keen attraction. And after spending a large part of the day with you yesterday, I have come to the realization that I don't want to spend a large part of any day in the future, without you. I know you are promised to another man, but I would ask you to reconsider. What I'm saying, Maryanne, is will you marry me?" He slid off the bunk and kneeled before her, offering her the flower, and looking up at her.

She had imagined this moment happening to her, from books she had read, and she had seen an ill-defined suitor, in her imagination, kneeling in front of her. The fact that she and Thomas had discussed marriage, by letter, in a cold and dispassionate way, was yet another reason that she had thought their relationship was doomed. Here was Peter, whose company she adored, and who now professed to adore her company too. There was really no other answer.

"Yes, I shall," she said simply, and took the flower.

Peter stood up, took her hands, and raised her to stand in front of him. "You have made me so happy!" He kissed her tenderly.

Maryanne's first kiss with another man was a defining moment in her life. She felt a thousand emotions all fighting for dominance in her heart. Love, happiness, relief, bliss, plus all shades and combinations of these. There was tumult in her brain.

Finally they sat down on the bunk together, holding hands.

Peter explained. "If our journey on this train had been longer, I would have given you more time to get to know me, before asking you. But as you know, we are due in Omaha tomorrow, and I would never have forgiven myself to let you disappear over the horizon without asking you. I am so glad I did!"

"I am glad you did too!" She placed her head on his shoulder, and experienced an all-encompassing feeling of peace and wellbeing. She was blissfully happy.

She and Peter spent the rest of the morning talking about their future. He went back to his compartment for lunch, and Maryanne remained in hers.

Chapter 9

After lunch, Maryanne decided that she had to tell George and Martha Thackeray about the situation, and request their assistance. She found out from the conductor where their compartment was, and made her way there. She knocked on the door.

Martha opened it. "Oh, hello my dear! How are you this fine afternoon?"

"I am well, thank you. May I have a word with you and George?"

"Certainly! Come in."

Maryanne sat on a bunk, and faced the two of them with trepidation. She took a deep breath.

"I have to tell you something that may shock you. And I also wish you to pass on a message for me." The two of them looked at her impassively. "I don't know whether you have noticed that I have been spending a lot of time with one of the soldiers on the train. He came to my rescue when we were ambushed by the Shawnee, and since then we have developed a relationship. He has shown me a side of life that I never knew existed, and I have to say that I have been swept off my feet!"

There was still no response from George or Martha. They simply listened.

"I have come to the very difficult decision to leave the train at Omaha, with Peter. That is his name. I had read about love at first sight, but I always thought that it was a fiction. However, it has happened to me, and it is very real! Peter has proposed to me, and I have accepted."

At this the older couple showed signs of life. They raised their eyebrows perceptibly.

"You may think it is foolish. I am sure you do. A girl like me, with no experience in the ways of the world, apparently throwing away a secure future for something that has no guarantees at all. You may be totally right. But I cannot deny my heart. If I were to stay with the train all the way to San Francisco, I should always pine for a life that I never had. I should be an unhappy and morose wife, which is not what Thomas deserves. He may not see it this way initially, but I really think that this is for his own good in the long run too. I came to tell you of the situation, since you had been kind to me and shown an interest in me. But in addition I should ask you a favor; that you inform Thomas of what has happened and explain it to him so that he may understand. Would you be able to do that for me?"

Martha took a long sigh. "My dear, I do understand. I have known of affairs of the heart. You are in the unenviable position of having two options, neither of which is ideal. As you say, if you were to carry to Thomas, you would always wonder what life with Peter would have been like. But at the same time, I am reasonably sure that you will find that life as a soldier's wife is far from wonderful too. You will never have enough money to live comfortably, and once the initial bliss has worn off, concern for money is all that will occupy your days. I just wish for your sake that you had had more experience of passion when you were younger. A heady romance or two satisfies the hunger for this sort of thing, gets it out of your system, and prepares you for settling down and embarking on the next loving phase of your life, which is that for your children, and which lasts until the end of your life."

George added "I am afraid that you are making a great mistake, but I can see that there would be no talking you out of it. I wish you whatever luck you can find." George seemed to be somewhat exasperated by Maryanne's decision.

Martha resumed. "We shall inform Thomas as gently as we can. I cannot guarantee that he will take it lightly, and I doubt that he will see that it is in his own interests. But we shall do our best."

Maryanne spoke "I shall also write to him, and set out my feelings as plainly as possible. But since you know him, I felt it would be so much better if you could explain the situation to him. Thank you very much."

Maryanne took her leave of the couple, who seemed now somewhat weighed down by the responsibility that she had placed on them. They did not look forward to having to disappoint Thomas at the station in San Francisco, as he waited there for his bride-to-be.

Chapter 10

The following morning, with a mix of apprehensiveness and happiness, Maryanne made preparations for disembarking from the train at Omaha. Shortly before they arrived there, Peter dropped by.

"Are you absolutely sure you want to do this?" he asked.

"Are YOU sure that you want ME to do this?" she countered.

"I couldn't be more sure of anything in the world." he replied.

"Then I am sure too."

He put his arms around her and they had a long embrace.

"I need to get back to my platoon. I'll see you on the station. I have arranged for your trunk to be removed from the baggage car."

"Thank you."

She sat and watched the passing scene show more and more signs of habitation, as they approached Omaha. Only two days ago she had wondered what this new phase of her life would bring. She could never have anticipated the right angle turn it was about to take.

They arrived in Omaha, and she alighted from the train. Her trunk was brought to her by two men, who asked her what she wanted to do with it. She asked them to take it to the waiting room. As she was following them, she saw George and Martha watching from the window of their compartment. She ran up to them. "Please try and understand! I know you think this is madness. And please try and get Thomas to understand!"

Martha smiled and said she would try. George couldn't manage a smile, even though he knew he should.

Maryanne met Peter outside the station. "OK, where to now?" she chirped happily.

"Just one item of business before we leave. Let's go to the ticket office and cash in the second half of your ticket."

"I didn't know you could do that!"

MARYANNE MAKES A DETOUR INTERRUPTED BRIDAL JOURNEY

They went and spoke to the ticketing clerk, and after he had conferred with his manager, they were paid out $80, half the original cost of the ticket.

Peter hired a carriage, and he and the two men loaded her trunk into it. He tipped them generously. He helped Maryanne up into the carriage, and took the reins.

"I know a very comfortable boarding house, that is only 3 blocks from the barracks. That's where you're going to be installed!"

They rode off into the town, found the boarding house, and Peter made the necessary arrangements with the landlady.

"You settle in here, and I'll be back in the morning, and we can start making arrangements for the wedding." He kissed her tenderly, and took his leave.

Maryanne unpacked her clothes, and had a long bath. She found that travelling by train had left her feeling somewhat grubby.

After her bath, she felt that she could put off no longer the two letters that she knew she had to write.

Neither was going to be easy, but she started with the one to Aunt Hilda, since she thought it would not be as difficult.

Dear Aunt Hilda,

I am sure you are wondering why you are getting a letter from me postmarked Omaha. I am afraid that there has been a change in plan. I'm sure you won't like it, but hopefully you will understand when you hear the circumstances.

On the train, I met a soldier from the Omaha barracks. He saved me from getting shot at by some Shawnee who ambushed the train. Since that time, he and I have been in almost constant company, and aunt, I have never felt as happy as I do with him. He is funny, considerate, adventurous (he took me on to the top of the one cars, while the train was going, and we even went through a tunnel!) and he makes me feel alive in a way that I have never felt before. He has proposed to me, and I have accepted. We are now in Omaha (he is still in his barracks, and I am temporarily staying in a boarding house), and very shortly we are to be married.

I can almost hear your exclamations of dismay as you read this. I know it must seem that I am very foolish, impetuous, and have no concern for the future. Those may all be true, but I could not carry on with the train after Omaha, and leave behind a life that, while possibly uncertain, offers adventure and thrill. You know the reservations that I had about Mr. Worthington. Life with him promised to be easy, but so dull!

Please do not think ill of me, aunt. I am sure that, if you had had the same upbringing as me, and were thrust into the same situation, you would have taken the same course of action.

Your loving niece,

Maryanne.

That wasn't too bad, thought Maryanne. Now for the tough one!

Dear Mr. Worthington,

I am sure that by the time you read this, you will have been informed by George and Martha Thackeray of the change of situation.

I am profoundly sorry for any hurt that this might have caused you, and please understand that, if there were any way that I could have done this without affecting you, I would have. However, I could see no such path.

My decision was not taken lightly, and I considered all angles of which I was aware.

The man I am to marry is kind, considerate and loving. He is all that I want. I am sure that a simple girl like me would have proved inadequate to your lifestyle requirements eventually.

I shall arrange to reimburse the $300 you sent me as soon as I am able to.

Yours with apologies,

Maryanne Marston.

She decided that she had better leave out any reference to the fun, adventure and passion for life that she expected with Peter, since it would have implied that she had no such expectations for her life with Thomas. It was the truth, but she didn't want to hurt him any more than she no doubt would shortly be doing. Also, she had promised to pay back the $300, but she had no idea where she would find the money to do so. She resolved to worry about that later.

After a light supper in the boarding house dining room (which, she reflected ruefully, bore no comparison to the luxury of the train dining car), she retired to bed, and dreamt of happy times to come.

Chapter 11

Peter came to the boarding house the next day, and they sat in the parlor. Men were not allowed into the single women's rooms.

"Right, Manny, we have a busy day ahead of us." He had already assigned Maryanne a nickname. She tried to think of a similar one for him, but could not come up with anything. "We need to arrange the preacher for the wedding, and then find a suitable house to rent."

"OK, I'm ready! Let's hit the trail!"

They went to a church that Peter had thought would be suitable, and spoke to the pastor. He agreed to perform the ceremony that Saturday afternoon. Then they started looking for a place to stay. That proved somewhat more difficult, since Peter's salary did not extend to anything other than the cheapest available, and there were not many that were available. However, they eventually found a very small rough clapboard single story house in a side street, that was just affordable, and was currently vacant, thus allowing them to have access immediately, and to move in right after the wedding.

They then had to find something with which to furnish it, and they discovered the difficulties of setting up home where neither had any family nearby who could have lent or contributed any items. They scoured the second hand shops and pawn shops for suitable pieces, with the refund from the train ticket coming in handy. After hiring a cart to move the items to the house, they eventually they had the rudiments of a home set up. They sat in the parlor, in two old chairs that they had bought, and surveyed the house.

"So, Manny my love, what do you think? Is this going to be enough for you? I know it's not quite the same style as Mr. Worthington would have provided, but it will be enough for us to start with, what do you say?"

"Please stop comparing yourself with Mr. Worthington! If I'd wanted to marry him I would have stayed on the train! I am here because I love

MARYANNE MAKES A DETOUR INTERRUPTED BRIDAL JOURNEY

you, and we are going to make a happy home here!" She got up and went and sat on his lap and hugged him. He returned the hug.

Over the next few days they returned to the house each day, to clean it up, add further smaller items of furniture, and generally make it into a friendly abode. Peter cleared some weeds from the garden and threw out some old rusty items that lay around. Maryanne managed to find some cheap material in a local haberdasher, and with it she sewed some curtains for the bedroom and the parlor. As each worked away, he or she would occasionally stop and look at the other, and feel that life was good. In the evening, in the boarding house, Maryanne added some frills to an existing white dress of hers, to make a passable wedding outfit. They waited impatiently for their wedding day.

Finally the day of the wedding arrived. Peter, with Stephen as his best man, arrived at the church in his best dress uniform, well in time. Maryanne had made friends with her landlady's daughter, and had asked her if she would be her bridesmaid. She jumped at the opportunity. They arrived at the church a little after the specified time, as is a bride's privilege. Without a father or any other male relative to give her away, Maryanne walked down the aisle alone. A few strangers had come to the church to pray, and they stayed and watched.

The ceremony went off without incident, and they finally walked back down the aisle as man and wife. The four of them went to celebrate at a local tea house, and had their fill of tea, coffee and fresh cream cakes. Stephen and the landlady's daughter seemed to get along admirably, and Peter winked at Maryanne when Stephen asked her if she would accompany him to an upcoming regimental dance.

After the tea, the happy couple walked to their new house. Peter carried Maryanne over the threshold, and then placed her gently down in the parlor. "So, what's it like to be Mrs. Simpson?" he asked.

"Mr. and Mrs. Simpson. It sounds wonderful!" They hugged each other.

Let us draw a curtain on our view of their lives at this point.

Chapter 12

Maryanne and Peter settled into married life in their little clapboard dwelling. Maryanne knew, from his initial description of his life as a soldier, that he would be away roughly half the time, on the train as it went from Omaha to Baltimore and back again, and she could accept this, since for the other half of the time, she had him to herself, apart from his occasional duties at the barracks. As a married man, he was relieved of some of these.

During the times he was away she busied herself with making the house into a home. She sewed, cleaned, and even learned how to paint the rather dull furniture which was all that they had been able to afford. She had learned the basics of cooking and baking from her aunt, but she now threw herself into becoming accomplished in this area.

During the times they were together they talked, laughed, went for walks, and reveled in each other's company. He showed her around his barracks, and she met Stephen again, who informed her that he and her ex-landlady's daughter were now walking out together. This made her glad; that the culmination of her and Peter's happiness had contributed to the happiness of two other people.

Maryanne felt that life could not make her happier. Until the day she awoke feeling a little odd. She had never felt this way before, and she had no idea what it could be. It was not that she was unwell, but something certainly was different. She put it down to something she might have eaten.

When the following day, and the next, it had not gone away, but had in fact increased slightly, she became a little worried. She went to see the doctor. He told her what her Aunt Hilda ought to have explained.

She got home, and it was luckily a time when Peter was home, since she didn't know how she would have kept the news bottled up for days if he had not been there.

She found him in the garden, planting some radishes. "Peter, love, you soon will have someone to help you in the garden!"

He stood up, and looked mystified for a second. But when he saw her unconsciously move her hand across her stomach, he understood. He dropped his trowel and enveloped her in a huge hug. "That's wonderful! I can't wait!"

They stood there in each other's arms. Maryanne thought back to her life just three short months ago, and how it had changed. She had found the man of her dreams, who had made her very happy. And now that she was to have a baby, her happiness was complete.

Printed in USA
Published by : Kent HamiIlton
© Copyright 2019
All Rights Reserved
No part of this publication may be reproduced or transmitted in any form whatsoever, electronic, or mechanical, including photocopying, recording, or by any informational storage or retrieval system without express written, dated and signed permission from the author.
By reading this you accept these terms and conditions.

www.ingramcontent.com/pod-product-compliance
Lightning Source LLC
LaVergne TN
LVHW041642070526
838199LV00053B/3523